Stand Like A Cedar

Nicola I. Campbell | Carrielynn Victor

HIGHWATER
PRESS

We went paddling in our cedar canoe
one rainy, spring day.
Pouring rain was fresh on our skin and we paddled anyway.
The rush and sweep of gentle waves
reminded us of the beauty of spring.

Who did you hear?

Swet he qeʔnimnxʷ

Íswȇł swam with us.
She shared a song
about her spring flight
returning from a long winter far away.
I am grateful for all newborn animals
making their first footsteps across the land.

Loon

I went gathering with my Yéye [grandmother]
one sunny spring morning.
When we arrived, the world was awakening to
the brilliance of the day.

Who did you see?

Swet he wiktxʷ

Springtime shoots and bitter roots
sprouting up from the land.
They shared a story about earth's transformation:
the end of winter and rebirth of spring.
I am grateful for the roots and shoots,
they provide the first springtime feasts for all living things.

I went running along a mountain trail

one blustery summer day.

land/earth
Tmíxw was warm beneath my feet

and sunshine glimmered through mountain leaves.

Who did you see?

Swet he wiktxʷ

snake

Sméyxł was resting on sun-warmed stones.
Sméyxł shared a story about her love
for her children and for summertime.
I am grateful for all living creatures, big and small.

I went berry-picking with my mother
in the highest, alpine mountains
one beautiful day in late summer.

Who did you hear?

Swet he qeʔnimnxʷ

A noisy clan of dusty, happy children.
A great caravan of family journeyed
from valley bottom to mountaintop.

We listened as our Elders shared a song about our ancestors
when they traveled by horse and wagon,
and before that by travois and on moccasin-covered foot,
in search of traditional foods to nourish our families.
We are grateful for the land that takes care of us.

We went fishing at our great river.
From the mountains our family went straight to the river
one beautiful day in late summer.

What did you eat?
Steʔ k Ʉupinxʷ

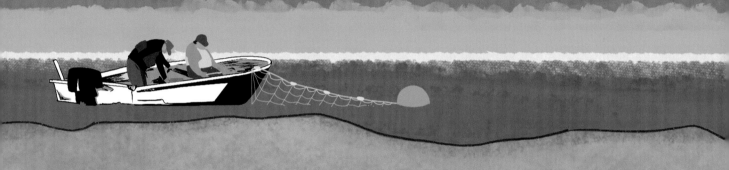

Five kinds of salmon came to visit us.
They shared a story of when our great river was clean.
We could walk on the backs of a million spawning salmon.
Our nets were always full and our children never hungry.

sockeye   chinook   coho   chum/dog   pink/humpback

Sxʷáʔes, kʷyíʔe, sxáyqs, kʷu úluʔxʷ, and héniʔ.

We took care of one another.

We are grateful for wind-dried, smoked, and jarred fish.

We went hunting one bright autumn morning.

Dad woke us before the sun rose above the mountains. He said,

"Wake up, my children. It's time for us to greet the day."

Who did you see?

Swet he wiktxʷ

Grandfather smíyc^{deer} visited us. His summer coat was turning greyish-brown.

He shared a story about his descendants and family.

He explained that death is part of our life cycle.

He said to honour our tears as though they were stars in the sky.

He reminded us to take care of the land.

I went walking one day in late autumn.

The world was changing to winter.

Snowflakes and golden leaves danced all around.

I needed to visit our sacred tmíxw, témexw, tmxulaxw.

(land/earth, land/earth, land/earth)

I needed to feel the cold breath of winter on my skin.

Who did you hear?

Swet he qeʔnimnxʷ

grizzly bear

A mother səxʷsúxʷ and her cubs crawled into their cave.
She shared a beautiful song about resilience.
I am grateful to walk in the footsteps of my ancestors.
Their courage to survive ensured our culture and traditions
will always be shared with future generations.

I returned to my favorite mountain trail
one sunny winter day.
Tmíxw was covered by a blanket of snow and ice.
I went anyway.

I needed to visit our sacred tmíxw, témexw, tmxulaxw.
I needed to feel the cold breath of winter on my skin.

Who did you hear?
Swet he qeʔnimnxʷ

raven   eagle
Great xláʕ and beautiful heléw'
sang among the cedars and douglas firs.

Together they danced in the sky.
I paid witness to their honour songs
that echoed tremendous love
for our tmíxw, témexw, tmxulaxw.

Today, we went to the lodge.
We went to the longhouse.
We went to the mountain.
We went to the land.
We went to the water.
We sat with our Elders and prayed.

We sang and danced in honour and gratitude of our loved ones.
This song is our promise to protect, honour, and respect:
 our sacred tmíxw, témexw, tmxulaxw;
the water that nourishes us;
the four-legged; the winged-ones;
the ones that walk and crawl.

We are Indigenous.
We love to run, paddle our canoes, dance, and play.
When we need to remember our promises,
we stand like cedar trees
hands raised to the sky.

We are grateful for all living things.

Glossary

Nłeʔkepmxcín phrases	English	Pronunciation
Swet he qeʔnimnxʷ	Who did you hear?	Shwet ha qahneem-n-xw
Swet he wiktxʷ	Who did you see?	Shwet ha week-t-xw
Steʔ k ʔupinxʷ	What did you eat?	Shtah k oopee-nexw

Nłeʔkepmxcín	English	Pronunciation
ísweł	loon	eesh-weh-lh
Yéyeʔ	grandmother	Ya-yah
tmíxw	land/earth	t-mee-xw
sméyxł	snake (garter)	sh-mey-x
sqyéytn	salmon (general term)	sh-q-yey-tn
sxʷáʔes	sockeye	sh-xwah-es
k'ʷyíʔe	chinook	kw-yee-ah
sxáyqs	coho	sh-xay-qsh
k'ʷu úluʔxʷ	chum/dog	k-wuh oo-luh-xw
héniʔ	pink/humpback	heh-neeh
smíyc	deer	sh-mee-ch
səxʷsúxʷ	grizzly bear	shux-shuxw
xláʕ	raven	x-lahh
heléw'	eagle	ha-la

Translation Guide

K/k enunciated at front of mouth. Kw or kw pronounced with a soft rounded mouth exhale.

Q/q enunciated at back of throat. Qw or qw pronounced with a soft rounded mouth exhale.

X/x enunciated, similar to clearing the throat.

Xʷ or xʷ pronounced with a soft rounded mouth exhale.

Ł or lh barred l/L or "lateral fricative" – enunciated with the tip of tongue on roof of mouth and a slow burst of air.

Stó:lō Halq'eméylem phrases	English	Pronunciation
Tewat kw'e ixw ts'lhà:m?	Who did you hear?	Tehwat kw-eh eexw
Tewát kw'e ixw kw'etslexw?	Who did you see?	Tehwat kw-eh eexw kw-ehts lehxw
Stám kw'e ixw lép'ex?	What did you eat?	Stahm kw-eh eexw lep-ehx

Stó:lō Halq'eméylem	English	Pronunciation
swókwel	loon	s-wok-wel
Sí:sele	grandmother	see-sil-ah
témexw	land/earth	tem-exw
álhqey	snake (garter)	alh-qay
sth'óqwi	salmon (general term)	s-th-eqw-ee
sthéqi	sockeye	s-th-eq-iy
tl'élxxel	chinook	tl-el-xel
kwōxweth	coho	kw-aw-x-weth
kw'ó:lexw	chum/dog	kw-aw-lexw
hō:liya	pink/humpback	hoh-lee-ya
tl'alqtéle	deer	tl-al-q-tala
kw'í:tsel	grizzly bear	kw-ee-tsel
skéweqs	raven	sk-ew-eq-s
sp'óq'es	eagle	sp-oq-es

Syílx (Okanagan) Nsyilxcən	English	Pronunciation
tmxulaxw	land/earth	tm-xu-lah-xw

To access additional resources, visit highwaterpress.com/product/stand-like-a-cedar or scan the QR code.

Coastal and Interior Salish Languages

There are approximately 203 Indigenous communities in British Columbia, with 34 distinct language groups. Indigenous languages represent the land, climate, cultures, and the voices of our ancestors. Indigenous people had no "border," and so the range of each group extends far across Turtle Island.

Due to colonization and Indian residential school efforts to exterminate Indigenous culture, and languages, most Indigenous languages in British Columbia are critically endangered.

Upriver and downriver Nłeʔkepmx, historically, referred to as "Thompson River Salish" traditional territory includes the Fraser Canyon, Nicola Valley, extending into the Similkameen Valley and Northern Cascades region of Washington State. The Northern and Southern Interior Salish language families includes seven distinct languages, and many dialects.

Halq'eméylem, is spoken by the Stó:lō, "People of the River." Hən'q'əmin'əm, is spoken downriver, closer to where the Fraser River joins the Pacific Ocean. Hul'q'umi'num' is spoken on Vancouver Island. The Coast Salish language family includes two dozen distinct languages and many dialects. Coast Salish Peoples have existed on Vancouver Island, Coastal Mainland, British Columbia, and Washington State since time immemorial.

This collaborative work represents a weaving of prayer, reverence, and tremendous love for s'olh temexw, tmíxw, and tmxulaxw. The health of all things in our environment will sustain a beautiful, abundant, and safe world for future generations.

We acknowledge the support of the Canada Council for the Arts.
Nous remercions le Conseil des arts du Canada de son soutien.

HighWater Press gratefully acknowledges the financial support of the Province of Manitoba through the Department of Sport,
Culture and Heritage and the Manitoba Book Publishing Tax Credit, and the
Government of Canada through the Canada Book Fund (CBF), for our publishing activities.

HighWater Press is an imprint of Portage & Main Press.
Printed and bound in Canada by Friesens
Design by Jennifer Lum
Cover Art by Carrielynn Victor

Kwuwscemxw and many thanks to Siyámíya Diana Kay, Mandy Jimmie, and Marty Aspinall.—NC

Library and Archives Canada Cataloguing in Publication
Title: Stand like a cedar / Nicola I. Campbell, Carrielynn Victor.
Names: Campbell, Nicola I., author. | Victor, Carrielynn, 1982- illustrator.
Description: Includes text in English, Nłeʔkepmxcín, and Halq'eméylem.
Identifiers: Canadiana (print) 20200294520 | Canadiana (ebook) 2020029461X |
ISBN 9781553799214 (hardcover) | ISBN 9781553799221 (EPUB) | ISBN 9781553799238 (PDF)
Subjects: LCSH: Animals—British Columbia—Juvenile literature. | LCSH: Animals—British Columbia—
Identification—Juvenile literature. | LCSH: Traditional ecological knowledge—British Columbia—
Juvenile literature. | LCSH: Ntlakyapamuk language—Vocabulary—Juvenile literature. | LCSH:
Halkomelem language—Vocabulary—Juvenile literature.
Classification: LCC QL221.B8 C36 2021 | DDC j591.9711—dc23

24 23 22 21   2 3 4 5 6

www.highwaterpress.com
Winnipeg, Manitoba
Treaty 1 Territory and homeland of the Métis Nation

With love, this book is dedicated to my children:
Myles David and Mariah Celestine.

NICOLA I. CAMPBELL

I dedicate this story to my Wyze Guy,
my greatest inspiration.

CARRIELYNN VICTOR